Legend

Legacy of Honor, Dignity, Kindness and Love

By

Magda Montasir

Dedication

To my late husband, my love, Dr. Mahmoud Dayar

your memory lives in every word I write and every dream I

chase. This book is a tribute to your strength, your kindness,

and the love that still guides me. May these pages carry a piece

of you into the world.

Magda Montasir

Acknowledgment

My deepest gratitude to The Times Publishers for believing in this work and supporting it with unwavering trust and to everyone who believed in my voice. Thankyou.

About the Author

Born and raised in Alexandria, Egypt, Magda Montasir graduated from medical school there and completed her residency at the same prestigious university. Afterward, she worked as both a practitioner and a teacher, contributing to the academic community. She was later granted postgraduate fellowships in both Germany and the USA, further expanding her expertise in the field. Fluent in four languages, she enjoys connecting with diverse cultures and perspectives.

Together with her late husband, who was also her classmate, she shared a deep passion for travel, music, and lively discussions about scientific issues. Their adventures around the world enriched her understanding of both life and science. Now residing in Newport Beach, California, she enjoys being close to the beach or any waterfront, where she finds peace and inspiration.

Though not a professional writer, Montasir considers writing a beloved hobby. She has previously published a biography and continues to explore the evolving field of medicine through her writing.

Table of Contents

CHAPTER ONE
THE FIRST FALL

There are moments in life that arrive without warning. They don't knock, they don't announce themselves, and they certainly don't wait for you to prepare. They simply show up, quietly, suddenly, and before you know it, you've stepped into a chapter you never knew you were meant to live. When I look back now, I realize that this is how love found me. Not gently, not gradually, not with reason or caution, but all at once, like stepping through a doorway I didn't know was open.

Some years ago, before life carried me into its new seasons, I sat down with a pen in my hand and a heart full of wonder. I wrote and published my biography, not because I felt old enough to record a life's worth of wisdom, and not because I believed my story was extraordinary. I wrote it because I had fallen in love, sincerely, unexpectedly, powerfully, and I wanted to hold on to every moment. It felt important then, like capturing sunlight in a jar before the evening arrived. I wanted a written memory of everything the two of us did together, every shared dream, every simple joy. Studying side by side. Planning with excitement for the next trip, the following year, the next possibility. Travelling together with the kind of eagerness only young love can stir. Laughing, discovering, and filling our days with the kind of happiness that has no pauses, no doubts, no second thoughts.

I remember thinking how strange it was that life could feel so different just because one person walked into it. And stranger still that I hadn't expected it. At the time, I had no intention of falling in love. I wasn't searching for anyone, wasn't hoping, wasn't waiting. Love has a way of ignoring intentions like that. It doesn't ask for permission. It doesn't wait until your thoughts catch up. It simply arrives, and you fall, helplessly, instinctively, without even realizing it's happening until you're already on the other side.

It's funny, the phrase falling in love. People use it casually, as though it's just another expression. But it's meaningful, more meaningful than I understood back then. You don't choose to fall. You don't plan to fall. You don't analyze it, or bargain with it, or map out the safest path. Falling is sudden, unthinking. One moment you are standing on familiar ground, and the next you are somewhere entirely new. That is exactly how it happened for me.

The first time our eyes met, something inside me shifted. I hadn't even spoken a word. I didn't know his name, didn't know where he came from, didn't know anything at all. But the heart often knows long before the mind catches up. Something about that moment, the way he looked at me, the quiet warmth behind his gaze, wrapped itself around me and held on. I didn't think, I didn't reason, and I certainly didn't choose. I simply fell.

If I close my eyes now, I can still see that moment as clearly as if it were yesterday. The room around us blurred into the background. His presence stood out like a light in a dim corridor, pulling my attention without trying. I hadn't felt that before, not with that intensity. And perhaps that's why it stayed with me all these years. A memory doesn't have to be dramatic to be unforgettable. Sometimes all it takes is one brief, quiet second that changes the direction of your life.

Back then, I didn't understand the language of love the way I do today. I thought love was something two people built over time, brick by brick, gesture by gesture, conversation by conversation. And perhaps that's true for some. But for me, love began with a fall. It began with a moment so natural and unplanned that it felt almost fated. I wrote my first book because of that fall. I wrote to remember the way his laughter felt like sunlight, the way our conversations seemed to stretch endlessly without losing warmth, the way we built our days together with a sense of ease and companionship that made the world feel softer.

Those early years were filled with small things, ordinary things, but they glowed with an extraordinary joy simply because we shared them. We weren't trying to impress each other or rewrite our personalities. We were just living, studying late into the night, debating ideas with the enthusiasm of youth, planning trips that felt like opening new pages in a book we were writing together. Even the simple act of walking side by side felt meaningful. I wanted to record it all because I feared losing any part of it to time.

The truth is, love transforms the everyday into something worth remembering. It makes you want to hold on tightly to life. And that's what I was doing back then, collecting our moments before they slipped away. The biography became a kind of time capsule, preserving not just the events themselves but the emotion behind them, the excitement, the companionship, the tenderness that shaped our shared life.

But life moves the way the tide does. It pulls you forward no matter how tightly you try to hold on. And although many years have passed since those early days of falling, the memory of them still carries a warmth that refuses to fade.

As I sit here now, writing again after so long, I think about that first story I told. I think about the girl I was then, full of love, full of hope, full of a sincerity that didn't worry about how it would be received. She wrote because she didn't want to forget. She wrote because love made everything feel precious. If I am honest, I envy her innocence sometimes. But I also admire her courage. She didn't hold back. She didn't question whether her feelings were too deep or too sudden. She simply accepted what life offered her and treasured it.

That first fall was the starting point. It shaped years of my life. It shaped who I became. And even now, long after time has carried me onward, I still believe in the truth of that moment. We don't choose who we love. We don't choose when love arrives. We only choose what we do with it once it's in our hands.

And I chose to write, then, and now, because some stories deserve to be remembered.

CHAPTER TWO
A RETURN TO THE PEN

Time moves differently when you're looking backward. It stretches and softens, blurring the hard edges of the years while sharpening certain memories into crystal. I didn't expect to find myself writing again after so long. For a while, I thought my first book had said everything I ever needed to say, at least about my own life, my own heart. I had closed that chapter with the quiet satisfaction of someone who wanted nothing more than to preserve a love story that meant the world to her.

But life has a way of circling back to you. Sometimes gently, sometimes insistently. And somewhere in the middle of ordinary days, between the routines, the responsibilities, the sunrises that feel familiar and the sunsets that arrive too quickly, I began to feel that old, persistent urge again. The urge to write. The urge to speak. The urge to remember.

It didn't come as a dramatic revelation. It wasn't born out of heartbreak, or triumph, or some grand moment of clarity. It was smaller than that. Softer. Like a whisper rising from a room I hadn't visited in years. A thought that lingered, it's time again.

At first, I brushed it aside. I told myself that life was too busy now, that I had said enough, that writing out of emotion belonged to a younger version of me. But the feeling didn't leave. It followed me quietly through the days. It nudged me during conversations, during quiet mornings, during the stillness right before sleep. And one afternoon, without ceremony, I found myself sitting down with pen and paper once more, almost the same way I had done years ago when love had first swept me off my feet.

Only this time, the story waiting to be told wasn't about romance. It wasn't about falling or flying or the warm glow of companionship. This time, the story came from further back, from my past, from my roots, from the people whose footsteps shaped the path I walk today.

It felt different, writing about legacy. Love had filled me with excitement. Legacy filled me with reverence. There are people in our lives whose presence is so strong, so full, so unmistakably bright that even after they're gone, they continue living in the stories we tell. And I realized, with a quiet certainty, that I owed it not only to myself but to those who came before me to tell their stories too.

I suppose age changes the direction of our thoughts. When we're young, we write to hold on to what's happening right now. When we're older, we write to remember what we've already lived, and what others have lived before us. That shift isn't sad; it's natural. It's the heart widening to include more than its own experiences.

When I began writing again, I wasn't the same person who had written out of love's first bloom. I was steadier, clearer, perhaps a little wiser. The years had given me perspective, not just on my own life, but on the lives that shaped mine. And so, instead of beginning with my own memories or achievements, I felt pulled toward something deeper: the legacy of a legend who had walked through the world with a presence that could not be forgotten.

It's strange how the mind works. You can go years without thinking of certain details, and then suddenly they rise to the surface with vivid color, the sound of a voice, the spark of a laugh, the way someone filled a room simply by being in it. I found myself remembering stories I had heard countless times. Stories told with humor, with pride, with that unmistakable warmth that belongs only to people who lived fully and loved wholeheartedly. Stories that carried his signature as clearly as a handwritten note.

At first, I hesitated. Writing about love had felt safe, even joyful. Writing about a legend from my past felt heavier, almost sacred. How do you do justice to someone who left such a deep mark? How do you put their presence into words when their presence was larger than speech?

But then I remembered something important: stories are not meant to be perfect. They're meant to be honest. And honesty was something he always carried with pride. So I pushed away the fear of inadequacy and let the words come the way they needed to.

What surprised me wasn't how much I remembered, but how much I felt. The memories didn't return like dry facts. They returned like living things, full of motion and color. His humor. His warmth. The way his eyes carried a spark that never seemed to dim. The way he collected people effortlessly, not through effort or charm, but through something deeper, something genuine. A kindness that didn't ask for anything in return.

When I started writing about him, I realized something else: the story wasn't mine alone. It belonged to everyone who had ever crossed his path. Each person who met him carried a small piece of his legacy, like fragments of light scattered across time.

And that realization carried me into the heart of this new book. It wasn't about preserving my life anymore; it was about preserving ours. His, mine, our families', our histories, our shared memories. The love story I had written long ago had been a story of two people. This new story would be a story of generations.

I felt a quiet responsibility as I wrote, one I hadn't felt before. When you write about love, you write from the heart. When you write about legacy, you write for the future. You write so that someone, someday, will pick up your words and understand where they came from, who came before them, and why those lives mattered.

In a way, returning to writing felt like coming home. Not to a place, but to a part of myself I had set aside. The part that believes stories are gifts, bridges that connect the living with the remembered. And as I wrote, I felt something settle inside me, something peaceful and sure.

It was time. Time to honor the past.

Time to speak the names of those who shaped my world.

Time to write again, not out of youthful love, but out of gratitude.

And so I turned the page, ready to begin the story of a man whose presence shaped an entire chapter of my life, and whose legacy still whispers through the years with the kind of strength only a legend can leave behind.

CHAPTER THREE
THE LEGEND

Every family has its stories, tales repeated over dinners, whispered in living rooms, shared in moments when memory feels heavier than the present. But every once in a while, if you're fortunate, a family doesn't just have stories. It has a legend. A person whose life rises above the ordinary, whose presence shapes more than one generation, whose footsteps leave marks deep enough that even the passing years cannot soften them.

When I began writing about him, I wasn't simply summoning memories. I was stepping into a world shaped by his shadow, warm, steady, unmistakably alive even now. His life had a way of stretching beyond its own timeline, reaching into the present with the same strength it had carried in the past. And the more I wrote, the more I realized that I wasn't documenting a single man's journey. I was documenting a force.

He was one of those rare people whose entrance into any room caused an immediate shift. Not because he was loud, or demanding, or dramatic. No, his presence had nothing to do with noise. It was quieter, stronger, a kind of gravity that pulled people toward him without effort. He didn't try to impress anyone, yet he impressed everyone. He didn't look for admiration, but admiration followed him naturally, like iron filings drawn to a magnet.

People talk about charisma as though it's a trick or a talent. But real charisma, the kind he had, was simply authenticity that didn't waver. It was the spark in his eyes, bright, alert, amused at life itself. It was the warmth in his voice, the easy humor that slipped into conversation without ever feeling rehearsed. It was the way he listened, really listened, as though every person he spoke to had something valuable to say. And perhaps that was his secret: he believed in people. And so people believed in him.

He collected friends the way others collect photographs, not intentionally, but naturally, simply by being who he was. Old friends, new friends, strangers who didn't stay strangers for long. Wherever he went, he left an impression. And that impression, people carried with them. They remembered his stories, the ones he told with such life that you felt as though you had been there beside him. They remembered his humor, gentle but sharp, playful but never cruel. They remembered the warmth that made you stand a little closer, laugh a little louder, smile a little longer.

He wasn't perfect, no legend is. But his virtues were countless. His generosity, his patience, his quiet strength. There was something about him that made people feel anchored. Safe. Seen. Loved. The kind of love that didn't ask questions, didn't set conditions, didn't fluctuate with the weather of life. His heart had a capacity that still astonishes me when I think about it. Not everyone is born with that. Some people learn to love over time. He seemed to be born knowing how.

And yet, despite all this, he remained humble. Deeply, genuinely humble. He lived his life without looking for applause, without expecting recognition, without carrying the kind of pride that often accompanies greatness. His virtue wasn't displayed; it radiated. There's a difference. And maybe that's why so many still speak his name with affection, even now.

But legends are mortal, too. And the day he left this world, the day his generous heart finally gave out, something inside all of us shifted. It felt as though a light had been turned off in a room we weren't ready to leave. His passing came with the kind of silence that feels heavier than sound. The kind you feel in your chest more than your ears.

I remember thinking how unfair it felt, how impossible it seemed that someone so full of life could simply stop. But that's the truth of life: it doesn't measure its endings by our readiness. And even though the world kept moving, even though the sun rose the next day and the next, there was a part of us that stayed frozen in that moment. Grief is like that. It pauses time even when life continues.

But his legacy didn't end with his departure. Legends don't fade; they echo. They travel from one person to another through stories, through memories, through the ways they shaped our character without even realizing it. If you listen closely, you can hear them still. In the way we speak. In the way we love. In the way we carry ourselves through the world with the quiet strength he taught us.

Sometimes I think about all the places he traveled, all the people he touched, all the laughter he sparked without even trying. And I realize that his life wasn't defined by the things he owned, or the successes he achieved, or the years he lived. His life was defined by the impression he left on hearts. And impressions like that don't disappear. They settle into the soul and remain.

As I wrote his story, I felt both the weight and the privilege of remembering him. The weight, because loss never becomes light. The privilege, because telling his story meant giving him a place on the page where time could not touch him. It meant sharing the truth of who he was with anyone who might read these words and feel even a fraction of the warmth he gave us.

He was more than the sum of his days. He was more than a memory. He was a presence. And presence, when it's as powerful as his, becomes a kind of quiet immortality.

He left this world too soon. He left with a heart that had given so much that perhaps it simply grew tired. But he did not leave empty-handed. He left us his example, his stories, his humor, his love. He left us a legacy marked not by wealth or titles, but by the way he lived, with boldness, with kindness, with a spirit that refused to dim.

And so, as I continue to write, I do it not with sorrow, but with gratitude. Because not everyone has the privilege of knowing a legend. And even fewer get to love one.

CHAPTER FOUR
A LIFE IN MOTION

A person's life is never just one home, one chapter, one setting. It moves, shifting, expanding, contracting, carrying us through rooms and landscapes that become memory long before we realize we've left them behind. When I think of his life, I don't picture a single house or a single stage. I see a series of places, each one holding its own story, its own rhythm, its own piece of who he was.

He lived fully, and his surroundings reflected that fullness. For years, his home was a four-bedroom house with wide windows that welcomed the morning light. Flowers framed the edges of the front yard, soft bursts of color that seemed to greet every visitor before he even opened the door. Tall trees stood like silent guardians beside the walkway, weaving their branches into a kind of natural arch as though nature itself wanted to honor the life unfolding inside.

In the back, the swimming pool sparkled with that quiet invitation only water can give, its surface catching the sky in every season, bright blue in summer, silver in winter. And beside it, tucked like a secret, was the sauna. That space became a sanctuary for many: a place for laughter, long talks, or simple silence. He knew how to make every corner of a home feel alive, as though the walls themselves were warmed by his presence.

But a single home was never the full boundary of his life. There was the beach house, salt in the air, waves murmuring against the shore, mornings colored with soft gold and evenings washed in deep blue. The ocean seemed to breathe with him, steady and sure. People loved visiting him there, partly for the breeze and the view, but mostly for the way he made even a simple breakfast feel like a celebration.

Then there was the desert home, a place so still and open that it encouraged reflection without even trying. The sky spread wide above it, the horizon stretching into quiet infinity. Some might find the desert lonely. He found it peaceful. He always appreciated stillness as much as he appreciated laughter, a balance many never quite master.

And of course, the lakefront home: five bedrooms, a billiard room, wide decks that looked out onto water that shimmered like glass in the early morning. I remember how the light played across the surface of that lake, how the gentle ripples carried reflections of trees and sky. That house felt like a retreat, a place where the world slowed down, where friends gathered not because of the luxury, but because being with him made any place feel welcoming.

But even with all these homes, life has a way of shifting its scale. Over time, he transitioned into something simpler: a two-bedroom condo high above the ground, the ocean stretching out beneath the windows, and the water channels winding like veins through the land below. Some might have seen it as downsizing. He never did. He saw it as another chapter, another view of the same world he'd always loved.

And that was who he was, never attached to the size of a space, only to the love within it. Hearts remained the same, even as the walls changed. Feelings stayed steady, even when the rooms grew smaller. What mattered wasn't the number of bedrooms or the square footage; what mattered was the life lived inside.

His life was never defined by possessions. Even in the grandest spaces, excess never touched him. What marked his journey was contribution, quiet, determined contribution that grew with every passing year. Research studies that pushed boundaries. Scientific publications that carried his name with respect. New procedures were developed with diligence and care. He gave, not to be recognized, but because giving was his nature.

In society, he was known not just for his accomplishments but for his commitments. Friends admired him not simply for what he did, but for how he lived. He nurtured relationships with the same devotion he offered his work. He remembered names, celebrated milestones, and showed up when others forgot. There was a steadiness to him that made people feel valued, a rare quality in a world that often moves too fast.

And then there was the devotion to his country, countries, really. He carried both with him: the one he was born into and the one he embraced later in life. He understood something many overlook: that identity is not diminished by adding another home. If anything, it grows richer. He was proud of where he came from and proud of where he chose to build the next chapter of his life. That dual belonging didn't divide him; it completed him.

His worldview reflected that blend. He believed in roots and wings, holding tightly to history while daring to explore new horizons. Perhaps that's why he connected so easily with others. Whether someone shared his background or came from an entirely different world, he found common ground. He recognized that every person walked with their own story, their own home, their own heritage.

Looking back, I realize that his life in motion was never about houses or travels or shifting addresses. It was about evolution, how a person grows, adapts, expands, and continues giving regardless of where they stand. His journey never narrowed. Even when the physical space became smaller, his heart never did.

And maybe that's the lesson hidden within his story: that life is measured not by the size of our surroundings, but by the size of our generosity, our spirit, our willingness to keep moving forward. He lived with grace in every stage, whether standing on a beach at dawn, resting in the quiet of the desert, laughing in the lakefront billiard room, or sipping coffee high above the ocean in that final condo.

He left behind much more than a list of homes or accomplishments. He left behind a blueprint: how to live with purpose, how to welcome change without fear, and how to love without holding back.

His life was in motion, yes, but always in the right direction.

CHAPTER FIVE
TWO COUNTRIES, ONE HEART

Home. It is a word we all carry in our hearts, though its meaning shifts with every step we take. For some, it is a street, a house, a town. For others, it is a feeling, a collection of voices, smells, memories that tie us to a time or place we may never fully return to. For him, for all of us who knew him, home was never a single location. Home was where the heart could breathe, where connection mattered more than coordinates, where roots and wings could exist side by side.

He understood something many of us forget: that being a part of more than one world is not a burden, it is a gift. Americans, after all, are a mosaic of stories, a patchwork of places we came from. Every newcomer brought with them the seeds of another home, another tradition, another way of seeing the world. And over time, all those stories blended into something new, a collective identity that carries the weight of many lands and the hope of many generations.

He carried that understanding in everything he did. It was not enough for him to live comfortably in a single place or to flourish in a single culture. He wanted to connect, to create, to celebrate the richness of difference. That vision is what led him, and a group of like-minded friends, to found the Egyptian American Organization. It was more than a club or a gathering. It was a bridge. A way to honor the past without losing sight of the present. A way to bring people together in celebration of shared heritage and enduring friendship.

I remember the early meetings, the excitement in the air as we planned events, dinners, and celebrations. We were a small circle at first, bound by a love for our origins and a desire to create something lasting in our new homeland. Year after year, more joined. New faces, new stories, new homes. And with each addition, the organization grew, not just in numbers, but in meaning. It became a testament to our resilience, our ability to carry old traditions forward, and to build new communities in the spaces where we now lived.

The milestones came quietly at first, then more prominently as the years passed. There were celebrations for holidays and anniversaries, gatherings that stretched late into the night. There were speeches, of course, and moments of reflection, but mostly there were stories. Stories of journeys across oceans, of challenges faced and overcome, of families preserved, of dreams pursued. And he was always at the center, not as a leader demanding attention, but as a guiding presence, someone who reminded everyone that we belonged not only to our past, but to the new world we were building together.

I think about that 40-year anniversary we celebrated recently, the weight of decades carrying behind it a quiet astonishment. Forty years is more than a number; it is a statement of perseverance. Of commitment. Of love, not romantic love, but a love that binds communities, that respects history, that honors everyone's journey. We didn't always recognize it in the moment. We were busy building, planning, and connecting. But when we paused to mark forty years, it was impossible not to feel the gravity of it all.

And yet, even as we celebrated together, the sense of home remained complex. "Back home" is something we often say without thinking. The words roll off the tongue as though the place we left behind still exists, still welcomes us. But home is not always a single point on a map. Sometimes it is an echo. Sometimes it is a feeling. Sometimes it is both. For all Americans who trace their roots to distant lands, home is a dual experience: it is where you began, and where you chose to continue. It is the past you carry, and the present you build.

He understood this duality instinctively. It was visible in the way he talked about our gatherings, our traditions, our achievements. He never allowed nostalgia to dominate; he never let pride turn into separation. Instead, he carried both histories with grace, honoring the land that gave him life and the land that embraced him later. To him, both were equally sacred, and both deserved celebration.

That perspective shaped everything he touched. When he spoke, it was never about possession, about claiming territory or asserting authority. It was about connection, about understanding that every person, every story, every home, carries meaning. That realization is what made him not just admired but deeply loved. People knew, without needing to be told, that he carried the weight of history lightly, but always responsibly. He reminded us that identity is not a chain but a tapestry, woven from every place, every story, every journey that brought us here.

Even as he grew older, even as his life became fuller with responsibilities, his devotion to this principle never wavered. He continued to foster friendships, to celebrate our origins, and to build a community that was inclusive, welcoming, and respectful. And in doing so, he left us a profound lesson: that home is never confined to one place.

Home is the heart we carry, the connections we nurture, and the legacy we leave behind.

I think back to all the moments when he would pause and reflect quietly, as if measuring not only his own life, but the lives of everyone around him. There was never judgment, only awareness. He understood the gift of belonging, the challenge of navigating two worlds, and the joy of creating bridges between them. Those who knew him felt it, not in speeches or proclamations, but in the way he lived, the way he welcomed everyone, the way he loved freely and without pretense.

Two countries, one heart. That is how I will always remember him. Not because it is an extraordinary feat, but because it is so rare. Rare to hold space for more than one place. Rare to belong fully to the past while building fully in the present. Rare to love with such generosity that every person touched by that heart carries a piece of it forward.

And so, as I write, as I remember, I carry that lesson with me. That home is both where we come from and where we choose to grow. That belonging is not tied to a single house, a single city, or a single nation. It is tied to the people we hold close, the communities we nurture, and the stories we carry. In honoring him, I honor that truth. And in telling his story, I hope others might feel the quiet power of a life lived with love for more than one place, for more than one world, and for every heart that was touched along the way.

CHAPTER SIX
HOME SWEET HOME

There is something about the word home that cannot be captured in a single definition. It is a place, certainly, but it is more than that. It is a feeling, a rhythm, a quiet understanding that no matter where you are, some part of you belongs to a particular space, a particular memory, a particular warmth that cannot be measured. Home is where the heart learns to rest, where it finds safety, and where it feels the subtle satisfaction of belonging.

I think that is why humans write songs about it, why poets turn to it again and again. Home sweet home. The phrase itself carries a kind of magic. "Take me home," the lyrics plead, over and over, in a way that resonates because it is a universal longing. There is comfort in the green grass at home, in the familiar corners of a room, in the echoes of voices we recognize even when years have passed. And we are not alone in this. Animals feel it, too: the birds returning to the same branches, the cats that know the exact spot on the windowsill where sunlight falls, the dogs that wait faithfully at the door. Home is instinctual, something stitched into the very fabric of life, not just human life.

He understood that instinctively. And perhaps that is why his presence made every place feel like home. It wasn't about furniture, or decor, or square footage. It wasn't about walls or doors or windows. It was about the heart he brought into the space, the warmth he carried, the unspoken care he extended to those around him. With him, a room became alive. A house became a shelter. A city became a place to belong.

And yet, there is a paradox in home, it is simultaneously fixed and fluid. We carry it with us, even when we leave. When we speak of "back home," we do so instinctively, even when decades have passed, even when the streets we remember no longer exist. Home exists in memory and in feeling as much as in bricks and walls. I remember countless conversations with him where he would pause, smile quietly, and say something about back home. Sometimes he meant the house he grew up in, sometimes the country of his youth, sometimes the people he had loved and lost along the way. And every time, the weight of those words carried more than nostalgia. They carried belonging. They carried life.

It strikes me as almost miraculous how home can be both private and shared. Each of us carries a personal idea of it, yet it is only made fully alive when it is felt together, with family, with friends, with community. Perhaps that is why the gatherings we held in his memory, and the celebrations he inspired, felt so profound. They were a reminder that home is a living thing, something we build with others, something that thrives in laughter, in care, in presence.

We celebrated forty years of the Egyptian American Organization a year ago, and I felt that truth more deeply than ever. Forty years of gatherings, traditions, and celebrations, all dedicated to carrying home across oceans, across borders, across generations. It was not just an organization, or a club, or an assembly of people. It was a living, breathing affirmation that home is not only where we start, but also where we choose to go, and who we choose to be along the way.

And yet, even amidst all of this, there is a simplicity to home that can never be fully expressed in ceremonies or speeches. It is the quiet moments. The mornings when sunlight falls just right across a familiar wall. The evenings when laughter spills from the kitchen to the living room and settles into hearts. The gentle rhythm of shared meals, shared stories, shared silence. That is the essence of home. That is what he understood. That is what he gave to everyone fortunate enough to know him.

Sometimes, I think home is a mirror; it reflects what is inside us as much as what is around us. When we are restless, it reminds us of stability. When we are joyful, it magnifies our happiness. When we are grieving, it offers quiet comfort. And he, in all his life and all his travels, always brought that mirror with him. He reflected care, generosity, curiosity, and love in ways that made everyone feel acknowledged, seen, and cherished.

The paradox of home is also its power: it can be everywhere and nowhere, constant and fleeting, simple and complex. I understand now why so many songs, poems, and stories revolve around it. There is an innate longing to find the place, or the feeling, that calls to the deepest part of the soul. And there is something profoundly human in recognizing that it is not only a destination, but a journey. A journey he lived every day, with every house, every city, every friend, every family gathering.

Even the smallest details mattered. He noticed the way light fell on a table, the aroma of bread baking, and the laughter of children in the yard. He understood that these ordinary moments, when appreciated, become extraordinary. That is how home is built, not in grand gestures, but in countless small ones, repeated with consistency and care.

Perhaps that is why I write now. Perhaps that is why I have returned to the page after so many years. To preserve the home he created, not just the physical homes, but the homes in our hearts. The sense of belonging. The warmth. The care. The quiet strength that made life richer, safer, and more meaningful. To capture even a fraction of that is to honor the legacy he left behind, a legacy that cannot be measured in bricks or rooms or addresses, but only in love, memory, and the hearts he touched along the way.

Home, I realize, is a story. And he was the living proof that stories matter more than walls, more than locations, more than possessions. They matter because they shape us, because they connect us, because they endure when we are gone. And so, as I close this chapter, I carry that truth with me: home is where love lives, where care is felt, where memory persists. It is eternal, as much as any legend can be.